FEEDING THE AFRICAN IMAGINATION

This Cassava Republic book belongs to:

_____

_____

_____

Mayowa and the Masquerades

Lola Shoneyin

Illustrated by Francis Blake

CASSAVA REPUBLIC
FEEDING THE AFRICAN IMAGINATION

Mayowa was looking forward to playing computer games all day when his mum said, "Remember we're visiting Granny in Ilisan this afternoon."

Mayowa did not want to go to Ilisan. He went to his room and sulked.

On the journey, Mum and Dad talked but Mayowa didn't join in.

Mayowa did not want to go to Ilisan. He went to his room and sulked.

On the journey, Mum and Dad talked but Mayowa didn't join in.

Instead, he looked out of the window at the
women selling food by the roadside.

When they arrived, Granny greeted Mayowa and his parents. "I have invited my neighbour's son to show you around," she said to Mayowa. "The masquerades are coming out today, so there will be lots of dancing. Denuyi! Denuyi!" Granny called.

Denuyi appeared with a big smile on his face.

As soon as they were on their own, Denuyi hopped after a grasshopper. Soon, the emerald green insect was sitting on his hand.

"It's beautiful!" Mayowa gasped.

The boys didn't want to damage its wings so they let the grasshopper fly away.

"Chasing grasshoppers under the hot sun is hard work," Mayowa said.

Denuyi took Mayowa to a stream. The boys perched on the water's edge and dipped their hands and feet in the cool water. "Let's hurry up so we don't miss the masquerades," Denuyi said.

"What are masquerades?" asked Mayowa.

"They are our ancestors. During the festival, they return to the world to dance with their loved ones."

"You mean we are going to see dead people dancing?"

"No!" Denuyi laughed. "Just wait and see."

The boys came to a clearing in the trees. "There's my father," Denuyi said.

"Baba," Denuyi called, "this is Mayowa. He has come to visit his grandmother and I am taking him to see the masquerades."

"I'm very happy to see you both. Before you go, come and have a look at these piglets."

Denuyi's father led the boys to a pig sty. There was a sow lying on her side, surrounded by tiny, pink piglets. Their tails were curled like pencil shavings.

As they continued on their way, Denuyi spotted a tall yeye tree. He helped Mayowa up the tree. They sat on a branch and popped the yellow fruits into their mouths.

"Listen, I can hear drumming and singing. It must be the masquerades!" Denuyi shouted.

The boys ran towards the music.

After a few hours, the boys found that they were all alone. The singing had stopped, the masquerades had left and all the drummers had vanished.

"Where are we? Do you know your way back?" Mayowa asked anxiously.

A man saw them and asked if they were lost.

"Yes," Denuyi whimpered. "We need to get back to Ilisan."

"Don't worry, it's not very far. Just follow the signs."

"Thank you, sir," Denuyi said.

Granny was the first to see the boys. "Welcome back. Did you have fun?" she asked.

"It was wonderful!" Mayowa's eyes danced excitedly.

"I've got to go now," Denuyi said. He waved goodbye to everyone and skipped out of the gate.

"Thank you for showing me around," Mayowa called out to him.

Granny led Mayowa to her garden.

"Ilisan is very quiet now. I feel sleepy," he yawned.

"Look at those birds," Granny said. "They are getting ready to go to sleep too."

"Look at my partridge pea plants. Their leaves are clasped together. Even plants know when the day has come to an end."

"Granny, I have seen so many interesting things today.

I can't wait to come back to Ilisan," Mayowa said.

Mayowa and his parents loaded the food that Granny gave them into the boot of the car. There was a huge hand of plantain, a bag of beans, dried fish, unripe mangoes and roasted peanuts.

"So tell us about your day, Mayowa," Mum said. Mayowa didn't respond. He was fast asleep with a big smile on his face.

A Cassava Republic Press UK edition 2016

Text © Lola Shoneyin 2010
Illustration © Francis Blake 2010

A CIP catalogue record for this book is available from the British Library.

ISBN:978-1-911115-14-4

www.cassavarepublic.biz

for Mayowa

who's got the biggest laugh of all

OTHER CASSAVA REPUBLIC PRESS BOOKS

And if you are interested in seeing the rest of our list,
please visit our website:
www.cassavarepublic.biz
www.twitter.com/CassavaRepublic
www.facebook.com/CassavaRepublic
www.instagram.com/cassavarepublicpress